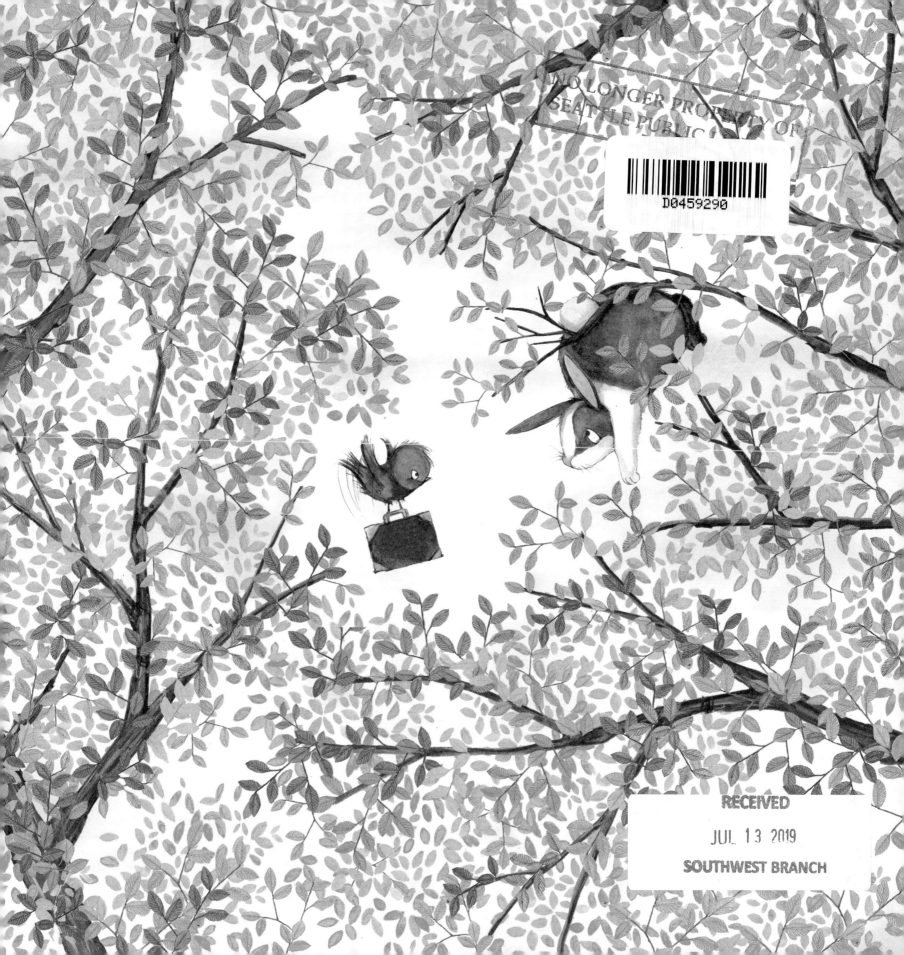

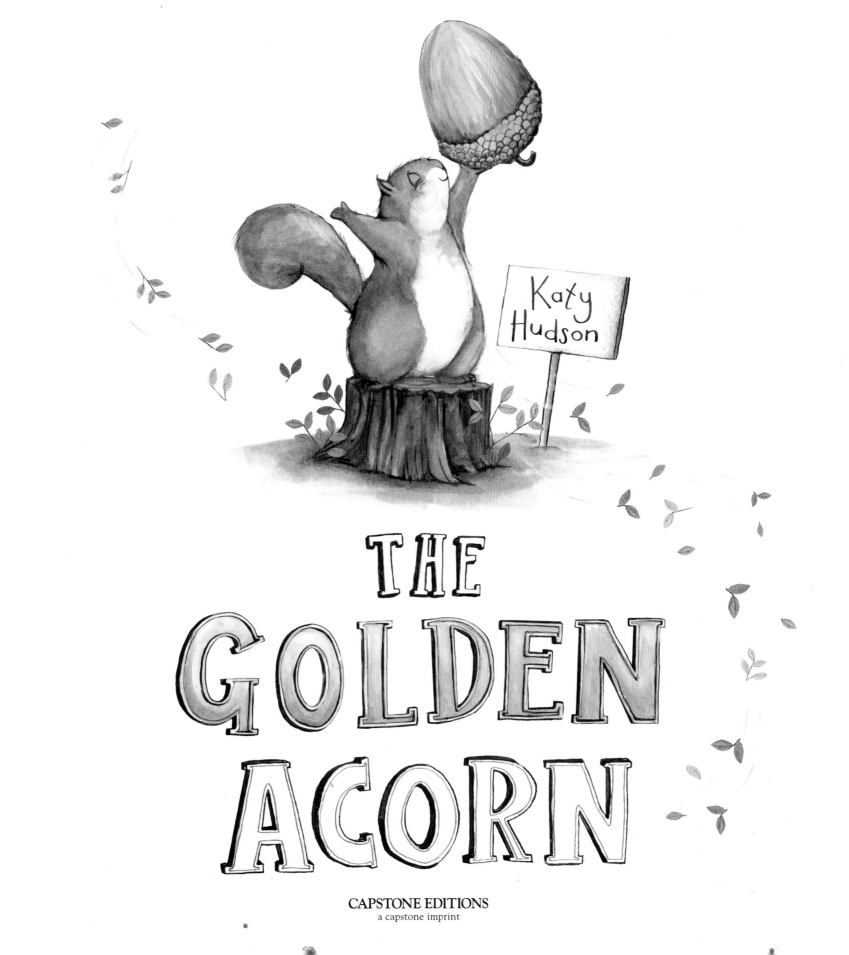

Katy Hudson

# THE GOLDEN ACORN

CAPSTONE EDITIONS
a capstone imprint

ONLY GOLD WILL DO

1

SQUIRREL
The Golden
Acorn Hunt

Grandma Squirrel
WINNER
OF THE
1st GOLDEN ACORN HUNT

Rabbit's
HOMEMADE
Carrot
Chutney

Squirrel's
EMERGENCY
BERRIES

Trophy
Care
Kit

FOOD
STORE

WINTER
FOOD
STORE

03
DAYS UNTIL
Race Day

1

GOLDEN ACORN
ELITE CLUB

1st
Place

The Golden Acorn
is published by Capstone Editions
1710 Roe Crest Drive
North Mankato, Minnesota 56003
www.mycapstone.com

Library of Congress Cataloging-in-
Publication data is available on the
Library of Congress website.

ISBN 978-1-68446-036-6

Summary: Squirrel wins the Golden
Acorn Hunt every year, but this year
the Golden Acorn Hunt is a team event.
Squirrel reluctantly enlists her friends
and is not impressed. Will Squirrel's
competitive spirit take over, or will
she learn how to be a team player?

Designer: Kay Fraser

Printed and bound in China.   1667

THE
GOLDEN ACORN
HUNT EST. 1928

THE FASTEST RACE
IN TOWN RETURNS

THE FASTEST ANIMAL
TO FIND THE ELUSIVE
GOLDEN ACORN
AND CROSS THE FINISH
LINE
WINS!!!

8x WINNER SQUIRREL TO RETURN
TO DEFEND GOLD TITLE!

For the
speediest
lady I know,
My Mum.

And for the
joy you bring,
my Mabel.
- K.H.

Eye on
the prize

Squirrel **LOVED** being the fastest. She could
fly through the trees faster than anybody
and had the trophy collection to prove it.

Her most prized trophies were from the annual Golden Acorn Hunt.

Only the fastest racers won the Golden Acorn, and Squirrel had taken it home the last eight years.

BUT THIS YEAR WAS DIFFERENT.

"All those competing in tomorrow's Golden Acorn Hunt must do so as part of a team," Beaver read.

Squirrel scoffed. "But I'm the fastest animal
in the forest! I don't need a team."

"But we'd love to be on your team, Squirrel!"
said Rabbit brightly.

"You?" Squirrel looked at her friends.
They really did not seem like race material.

But Squirrel had no choice. The race was tomorrow.
Maybe a little training would do the trick . . .

. . . OR MAYBE NOT.

The next morning,
Squirrel gathered her
team at the starting line.

"The Golden Acorn has been
hidden," the judge yelled.
"READY! SET! GO!"

**WHOOSH!** Squirrel was off, overtaking all the other racers—even her own team!

"Squirrel, wait!" her friends called. "We've lost Tortoise!"

"Ugh, Tortoise," huffed
Squirrel, pacing back.

Squirrel grabbed Tortoise, plopped him back on the branch, and took off again—but not for long.

"Squirrel, wait!" her friends called once more. "We're all tangled up."

Squirrel untangled her friends and was off yet again—for about ten seconds.

"You can't
be serious,"
Squirrel moaned.

"Squirrel,
wait!" her
friends called.
"Beaver is
stuck!"

"Oh, come on!"
Squirrel groaned.

Once Beaver's bottom was pushed free, Squirrel was off as fast as her feet would carry her—so fast that she didn't even hear her friends calling for her.

Over logs and under branches.
Inside trunks and above treetops.
Squirrel raced as fast as she could
to find the Golden Acorn. Until . . .

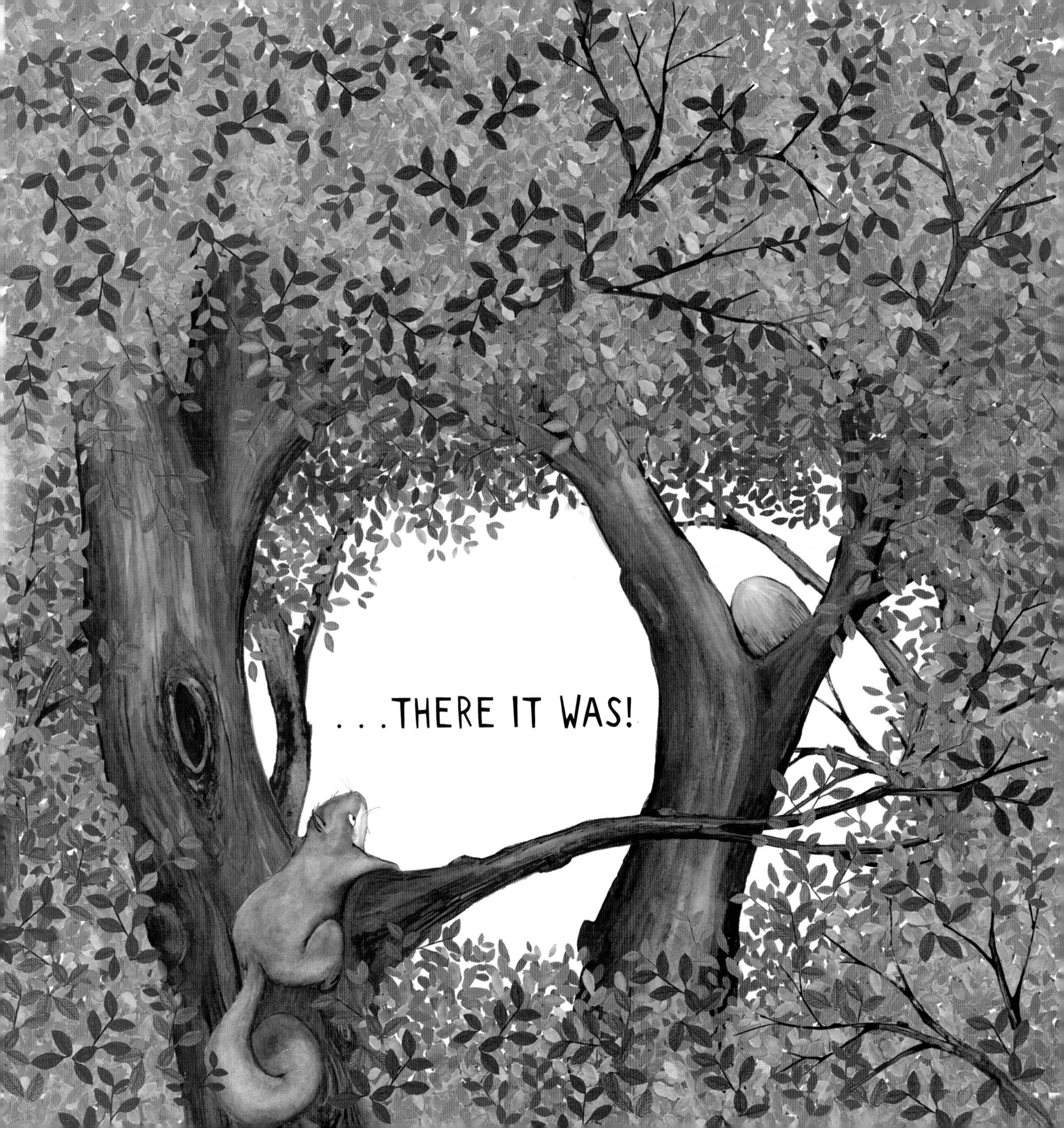

. . . THERE IT WAS!

It was the biggest Golden Acorn
Squirrel had ever seen! She pried it
from its hiding spot and took off.

But the Golden Acorn was heavy.
Much too heavy to carry alone.

And there was only Squirrel—all by
herself. Squirrel and her golden prize.

After lots and lots of rolling
and pushing and heaving,
she took a little rest. She
was tired and sweaty and . . .

. . . lonely.

And as Squirrel looked out upon all the
other racers, still searching for the acorn,
she realized she had lost her friends.
The Golden Acorn would just have to wait.

**WHOOSH!** Off Squirrel raced, faster than
she ever had before. Over logs, under branches,
inside trunks, and above the treetops until . . .

. . . THERE THEY WERE!

After lots and lots of rolling
and pushing and heaving,
Squirrel had her friends back.

Her team didn't come
in first, and they didn't get
a trophy. But it didn't matter.

From now on Squirrel's friends would **ALWAYS** come first.